LITTLE BEAR'S FRIEND

An I CAN READ Book

by ELSE HOLMELUND MINARIK

pictures by MAURICE SENDAK

HEINEMANN · LONDON

First published in Great Britain 1961 by
World's Work Ltd
Reissued 1992 by William Heinemann Ltd,
Michelin House, 81 Fulham Road, London SW3 6RB

LONDON MELBOURNE AUCKLAND

0 434 96175 2

Produced by Mandarin Offset
Printed in Hong Kong

To

Mother and Father

CONTENTS

LITTLE BEAR AND EMILY

Little Bear sat in the top

of a high tree.

He looked all around him

at the wide, wide world.

He saw the green hills.

He saw the river.

And far, far away

he saw the blue sea.

He saw the tops of trees.

He saw his own house.

He saw Mother Bear.

He could hear the wind sing.

And he could feel the wind

on his fur, on his eyes,

on his little black nose.

He shut his eyes,

and let the wind brush him.

He opened his eyes,

and saw two little squirrels.

"Play with us," they said.

"No time," said Little Bear.

"I have to go home for lunch.'

13

He began to climb down,

and saw four little birds.

"Look at us," they said,

"we can fly."

"I can, too," said Little Bear,

"but I always fly down.

I can't fly up

or sideways."

He climbed down a bit further
and saw a little green worm.

"Hello," said the little green worm.

"Talk to me."

"Some other time," said Little Bear.

"I have to go home for lunch."

He climbed all the way down,

and there he saw a little girl.

"I think I am lost,"

said the little girl.

"Could you see the river

from the treetop?"

"Oh, yes," said Little Bear,

"I could see the river.

Do you live there?"

19

"Yes," said the little girl.

"My name is Emily.

And this is my doll Lucy."

"I am Little Bear, and
I can take you to the river.
What is in that basket?"

"Biscuits," said Emily. "Have some."

"Thank you. I love biscuits."

"So do I," said Emily.

They walked along eating biscuits
and talking,
and soon they came to the river.

"I see our tent," said Emily,
"and my mother and father."

"And I hear my mother calling,"

said Little Bear.

"I have to go home for lunch.

Good-bye, Emily."

22

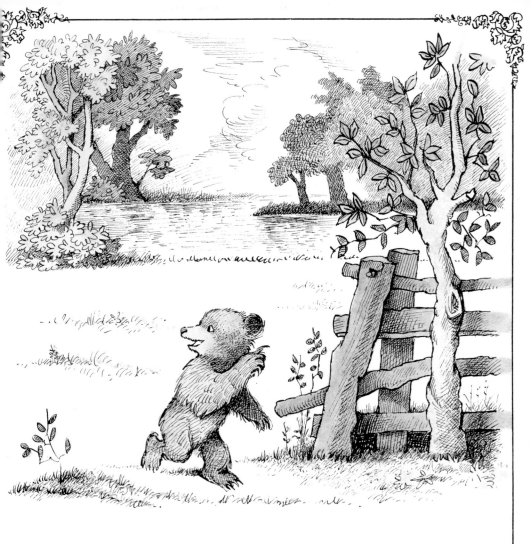

"Good-bye, Little Bear.

Come back and play with me."

"I will," said Little Bear.

23

Little Bear went skipping home.

He hugged Mother Bear and said,

"Do you know what I just did?"

"What did you just do, Little Bear?"

24

"I climbed to a treetop,

and I saw the wide world.

I climbed down again, and I saw

two squirrels, four little birds

and a little green worm.

Then I climbed all the way down,

and what do you think I saw?"

"What did you see?"

"I saw a little girl named Emily.

She was lost, so I helped her

to get home.

And now I have a new friend.

Who do you think it is?"

"The little green worm,"
said Mother Bear.

Little Bear laughed.

"No," he said, "it is Emily.
Emily and I are friends."

DUCK, BABY-SITTER

Owl was having a party.

Little Bear, Emily and Lucy

were on the way to Owl's house.

They came to the pond

where Duck lived.

And there was Duck,

baby-sitting.

Little Bear looked at

all the ducklings.

"My goodness!" said Duck.

"I think I have lost one!"

Little Bear and Emily

began to look for it.

Little Bear looked at

the tall reeds.

He said,

"If I were a duckling,

that is where I would swim.

It would be like swimming

in a forest."

He looked in the tall reeds.

And there was the duckling,

swimming about,

having fun.

"Hello, Little Cheep,

I see you,"

said Little Bear.

"Cheep!" said the duckling,

and swam out to the others.

Just in time, too,

because his mother had come back.

"Hooray!" said Duck.

"Now I am free.

Now we can go to the party."

They went skipping along.

Emily said,

"I think ducklings are lovely."

"Yes," said Little Bear,

"and owlets are nice, too.

Owl says they are."

Emily laughed.

"Oh," she said,

"I love all little animals."

Cat looked at Lucy.

"Who is that?" he said.

"That is Lucy," said Little Bear.

"Lucy is Emily's doll."

"Yes," said Emily.

"And she tells me things.

She wants to tell me something now."

"What?" said Cat.

"I can't hear her."

Emily put her head down
to Lucy's head.

"What is she saying?" asked Hen.

"Yes, tell us," said Duck.

"She is saying," said Emily,
"that she wants to sit up here."
And Emily made Lucy sit
in a little tree.

"There!" said Little Bear.
"Emily knows what Lucy wants."

"Let's start," said Cat.

Owl came out of his house.

He said,

"Here are the party hats.

Put them on."

So they all put on party hats

and laughed at each other.

Then they sat down to eat.

"Look at Lucy!" said Duck.

"She wants to come down!"

They all looked, and there was Lucy,

coming down all by herself.

"Oh—Oh!" cried Emily.

"Lucy will break."

And Lucy did break.

She broke her arm.

"Oh, Lucy!"

Emily was crying.

She picked up her doll,

and hugged her.

"Don't cry, Emily," said Little Bear,

"we can mend her."

"I'll get some sticky tape," said Owl.

So Little Bear mended Lucy.

"There," he said.

"Ask her how she feels now."

Emily put her head down to Lucy

"She says she feels better,"
said Emily.
"And she says you are
a very good doctor, Little Bear."

"That's kind of her,"
said Little Bear.
"Any time she breaks an arm,
or a leg, I will mend it."

Owl laughed.

"No more today, please,"

he said.

Emily made Lucy sit down.

Hen asked,

"Is she saying something?"

"Yes," said Emily,

"she wants us to begin the party."

And that is just what they did.

It was a very fine party indeed,

even for Lucy.

She said so herself.

"YOUR FRIEND, LITTLE BEAR"

Summer was over,

and Emily was saying good-bye.

It was time to go

back to school.

Mother Bear baked a cake.

Little Bear made lemonade.

Mother Bear said,

"Let us eat up all the cake.

If we do, then it will not

rain tomorrow."

"Let it rain," said Little Bear.

"Emily will not be here tomorrow

to play with me."

"Anyhow," said Emily,

"we can eat up the cake.

And we can drink the lemonade."

So they ate the cake,

and drank the lemonade,

and talked and talked.

Then it was time

for Emily to go home.

51

Father Bear said,

"Don't let Lucy break

any more arms."

"Oh, no," said Emily.

Emily hugged her doll, and said,

"Lucy wants to say good-bye, too.

Say good-bye to Little Bear, Lucy."

Emily made Little Bear hold Lucy.

53

Then she said to him,

"Little Bear, you can have Lucy

for keeps.

I will give her to you."

"Oh—" began Little Bear.

54

But before he could say anything,

Emily took Lucy back again.

"Oops!" she said. "I forgot.

Lucy has to come to school with me."

Emily opened her purse

She took out a fine new pen.

"This is for you," she said.

"I want you to have it."

Little Bear took the pen.

"Thank you, Emily," he said.

She took Little Bear's paw in hers,

and helped him to begin—

That made Little Bear very happy.

He said,

"When can I write to Emily?"

"Soon," said Mother Bear.

And soon he did write to Emily,
like this:

Dear Emily:

It is snowing.

I love the snow.

I wish I could send you some.

Owl, Duck, Hen and Cat

send their love.

So do the ducklings.

I cannot wait for summer.

Your friend,

Little Bear.